This book belongs to

Name................................

Age.............

Thomas
the Tank Engine

Story Collection

EGMONT
We bring stories to life

First published in Great Britain in 2017 by Egmont UK Limited,
The Yellow Building, 1 Nicholas Road, London W11 4AN

The Story of Thomas the Tank Engine first published in 2015, written by Ronne Randall,
based on *Thomas the Tank Engine* first published in Great Britain in 1946
A Visit to London for Thomas the Tank Engine first published in 2016, written by Ronne Randall
Three Cheers for Thomas the Tank Engine first published in 2015, written by Joseph Marriott
and Jane Riordan

Designed by Martin Aggett
Stories illustrated by Robin Davies
Map illustration by Dan Crisp

 Thomas the Tank Engine & Friends™

CREATED BY BRITT ALLCROFT

Based on the Railway Series by the Reverend W Awdry
© 2017 Gullane (Thomas) LLC. Thomas the Tank Engine & Friends and
Thomas & Friends are trademarks of Gullane (Thomas) Limited.
Thomas the Tank Engine & Friends and Design is Reg. U.S. Pat. & Tm. Off.
© 2017 HIT Entertainment Limited.

ISBN 978 1 4052 8772 2
66569/1

Printed and bound in EU

Stay safe online. Any website addresses listed in this book are correct
at the time of going to print. However, Egmont is not responsible for content
hosted by third parties. Please be aware that online content can be subject
to change and websites can contain content that is unsuitable for children.
We advise that all children are supervised when using the internet.

Thomas
the Tank Engine

Story Collection

CONTENTS

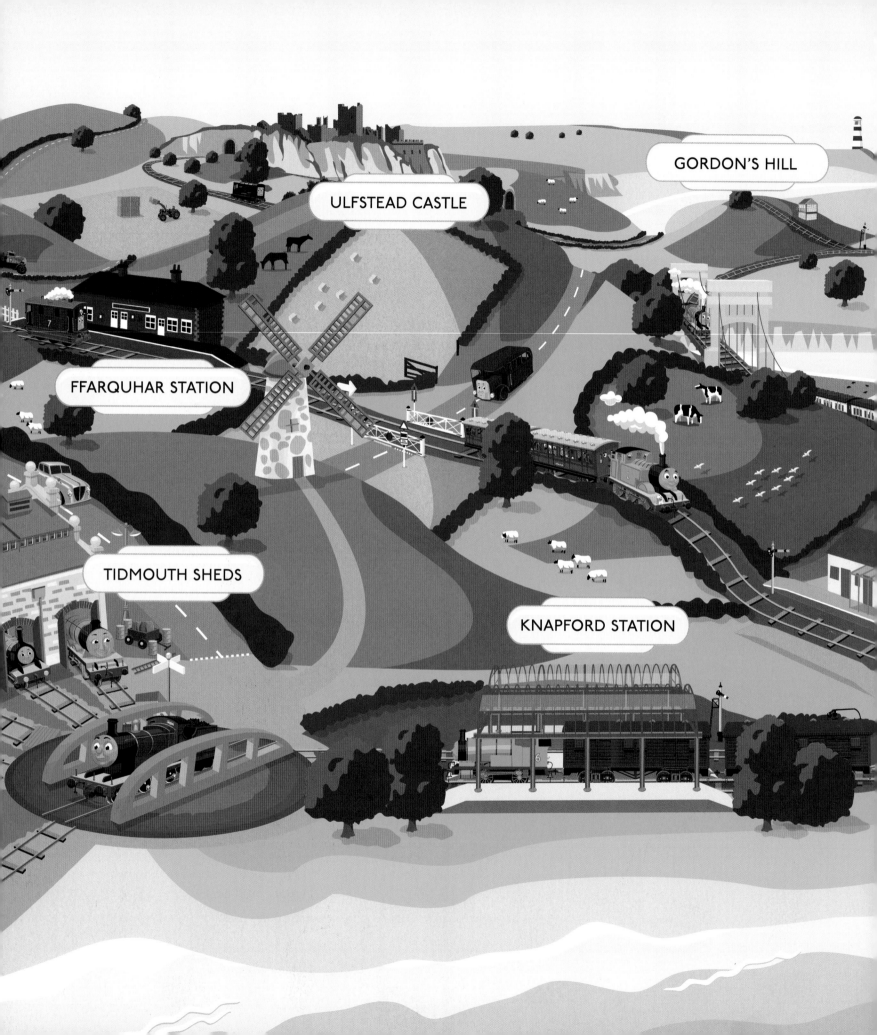

GORDON'S HILL

ULFSTEAD CASTLE

FFARQUHAR STATION

TIDMOUTH SHEDS

KNAPFORD STATION

CHINA CLAY PITS

BRENDAM DOCKS

DRYAW STATION

THE ISLAND OF SODOR

THE STORY OF
Thomas the Tank Engine

This is a story about Thomas the Tank Engine, who worked with his engine friends on The Fat Controller's Railway on the Island of Sodor.

Thomas the Tank Engine was a cheeky little engine who helped the big engines by pulling their coaches to and from the **BIG** Station.

But what Thomas really wanted was his very own Branch Line. That way he would be a **Really Useful Engine**.

Sometimes Thomas liked to play tricks on the other engines.

One day, when Gordon, the **BIG STRONG** engine, was very tired from pulling the heavy Express train, Thomas came up beside him and whistled loudly.

"PEEP! PEEP!

WAKE UP, LAZYBONES!"

That gave Gordon a fright! He decided to teach cheeky Thomas a lesson.

The next morning, Thomas would
not wake up. It was nearly time
for Gordon's Express to leave,
and Thomas hadn't got his
coaches ready.

"Yaa-aaw-n,"

said Thomas,
getting started at last.

"Hurry up, Thomas!" said Gordon crossly.

Thomas' job was to push Gordon's train to help him start.

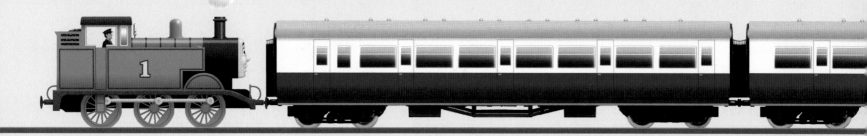

As he moved out of the
station, he started to
go *faster* and *faster*.

Faster and **faster** and **faster** and **faster** went Gordon.

It was much too **fast** for Thomas!

That morning was Gordon's chance to teach Thomas a lesson.

"Hurry, hurry, hurry, hurry!" laughed Gordon.

Poor Thomas was going **faster** than he had ever gone before.

"My wheels will wear out!" he thought.

"Peep! Peep!

Stop! Stop!"

whistled Thomas.

21

At last they stopped at a station.

"Well, Thomas," chuckled Gordon.
"Now you know how it feels
to be tricked!"

"**Puff!**
Puff!"
panted poor Thomas.

He was too out of breath to say anything.
His cheekiness had got him into trouble.
Perhaps he would never get his
own Branch Line now.

The next day, Thomas saw some strange-looking trucks in the Yard.

"That's the breakdown train," said his Driver. "It helps out when there's an accident."

Just then, James, the Splendid Red Engine, came through the Yard crying.

His trucks were pushing him too **fast**, and his brake blocks were on fire!

"HELP! HELP!"

25

Soon after James disappeared, a man came running.

"James is off the line! We need the breakdown train – quickly!" he shouted.

Thomas was coupled on to the breakdown train, and off he went as **fast** as he could.

Whirrrrrr went his wheels along the track.

"I must help James," he said.

They found James in a field, with the trucks piled in a heap behind him. His Driver and Fireman were checking that he was all right.

"It wasn't your fault, James," his Driver said.
"It was those Troublesome Trucks!"

James needed help. Thomas pushed the breakdown train alongside James.

Then he pulled some trucks out of the way.

He was soon back to pick up the rest.

"Oh... dear!
Oh... dear!"
they groaned.

"Serves you right. Serves you right," puffed Thomas crossly. He worked hard all afternoon.

Thomas pulled James back to the Shed, where The Fat Controller was waiting.

"Well, Thomas," he said, "you have shown that you're a **Really Useful Engine**. I'm so pleased with you that I'm going to give you your own Branch Line."

"Oh, thank you, Sir!"
said Thomas happily.

Now Thomas is happy as can be, and he **chuffs** and **puffs** proudly along his own Branch Line from morning till night.

Gordon is always in a hurry, but whenever he sees Thomas he remembers to say, **"Hurry! Hurry!"** And cheeky little Thomas always whistles,

"PEEP! PEEP!

Lazybones!"

A Visit to London for Thomas the Tank Engine

This is a story about how Thomas the Tank Engine helped The Fat Controller have a very special day in London!

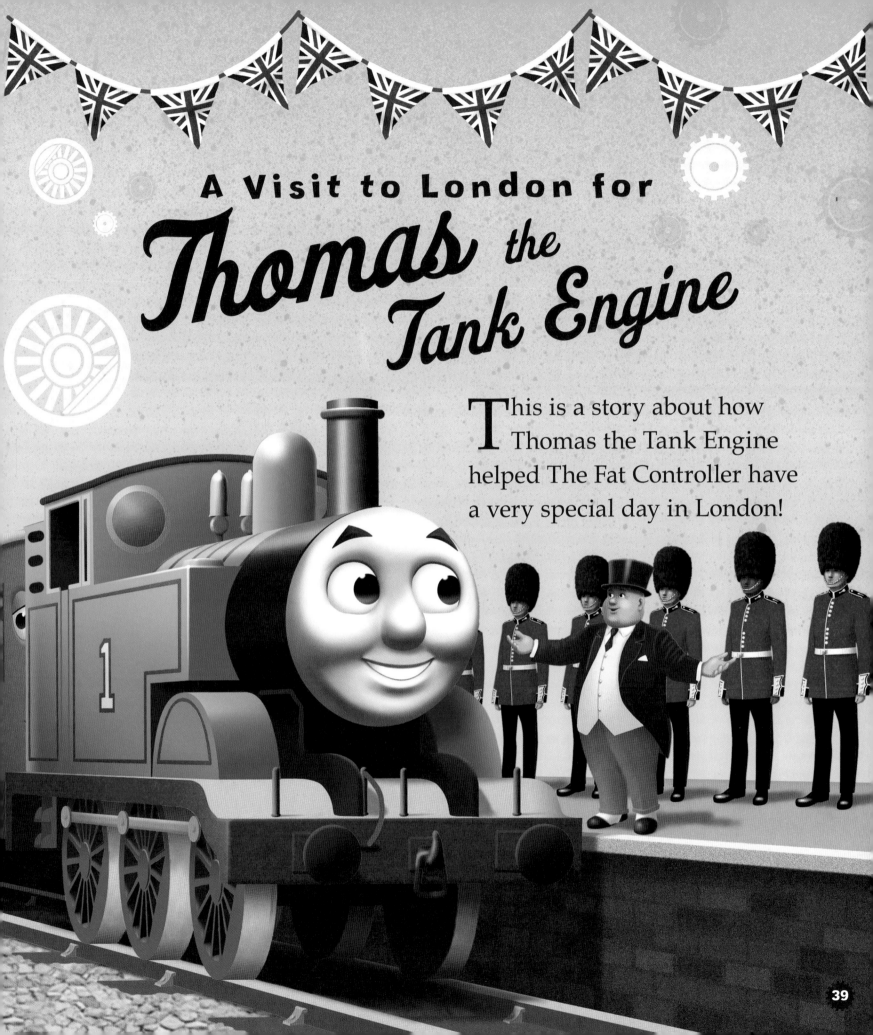

Thomas the Tank Engine and Henry, Gordon and Edward were all shiny and polished. Their Drivers wanted them to look their best.

The Fat Controller was going to choose one of them to do a very special job!

The Fat Controller
inspected each engine.

Finally he announced, "Thomas, I choose you to take me and Lady Hatt to London to meet the **Queen!** We must get to Big Ben at four o'clock for the start of her birthday celebrations."

None of the engines were sure who Big Ben was but Thomas shivered with excitement. He would be meeting the Queen and going to London, the biggest city in the land!

The next morning, Thomas was coupled up to Annie, who carried The Fat Controller and Lady Hatt.

They chugged off to Brendam Docks, where Cranky was waiting to put them on the ferry to the Mainland.

"That ferry is late again!" said Cranky crossly. "You'll have to hurry if you want to arrive in London on time."

On the Mainland, Thomas puffed through the countryside…

…and past a big train going the other way.
"Peep! Peep!" called Thomas.
"Wheeeeeeeee!" the train whistled back.

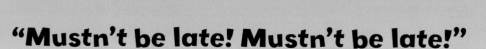

"Mustn't be late! Mustn't be late!"
Thomas puffed. "It's already two o'clock."

"Hurry! Hurry! Hurry!" he panted as, at last, roofs and chimneys came into sight.

"Good work, Thomas!" said his Driver.
"We've arrived in Greenwich. That building is
the Royal Observatory. They have a telescope
there that can see all the way to the stars!"

"Can it see as far as Sodor?"
Thomas asked.

"Much further!" laughed his Driver.

At the River Thames, Thomas was told that they would be finishing the journey by boat.

Thomas saw a big sailing ship. "Is that the boat?" he wondered.

"No," said his Driver, smiling. "That is a very old ship called the *Cutty Sark*. It used to bring tea all the way from China."

Thomas had never heard about so many faraway places in just one day!

All at once there was a merry **TOOT! TOOT!**

"I'm Dilly," said a friendly barge. "I'll take you into London and show you some sights along the way!"

"It's three o'clock," Thomas said nervously. "We mustn't be late for the Queen and Big Ben!"

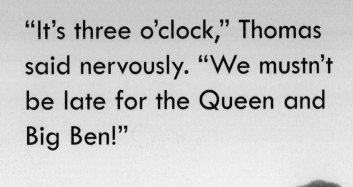

"I'll have you there quicker than you can say 'Piccadilly Circus!'" Dilly promised.

With Thomas and Annie
safely aboard, Dilly set off.
A big bridge loomed up in
front of them. To Thomas'
amazement, it opened up
to let them through!

"This is Tower Bridge,"
Dilly told him. "And there
is the Tower of London.
It's almost a thousand
years old!"

"The dome is St Paul's Cathedral," Dilly said. "It was built after the Great Fire of London, more than three hundred years ago."

"That's The Shard," said Dilly. "It's the tallest building in England!"

"That big wheel is the London Eye,"
Dilly went on. "From the top you
can see all over London!"

"These are the Houses of Parliament,"
Dilly explained. "This is where laws are
made. And there is the Elizabeth Tower,
with its huge bell, Big Ben."

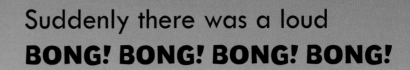

Suddenly there was a loud
BONG! BONG! BONG! BONG!

"Four o'clock!" said Dilly. "We're right on time!"

"So that's Big Ben," laughed Thomas looking up at the big clock.

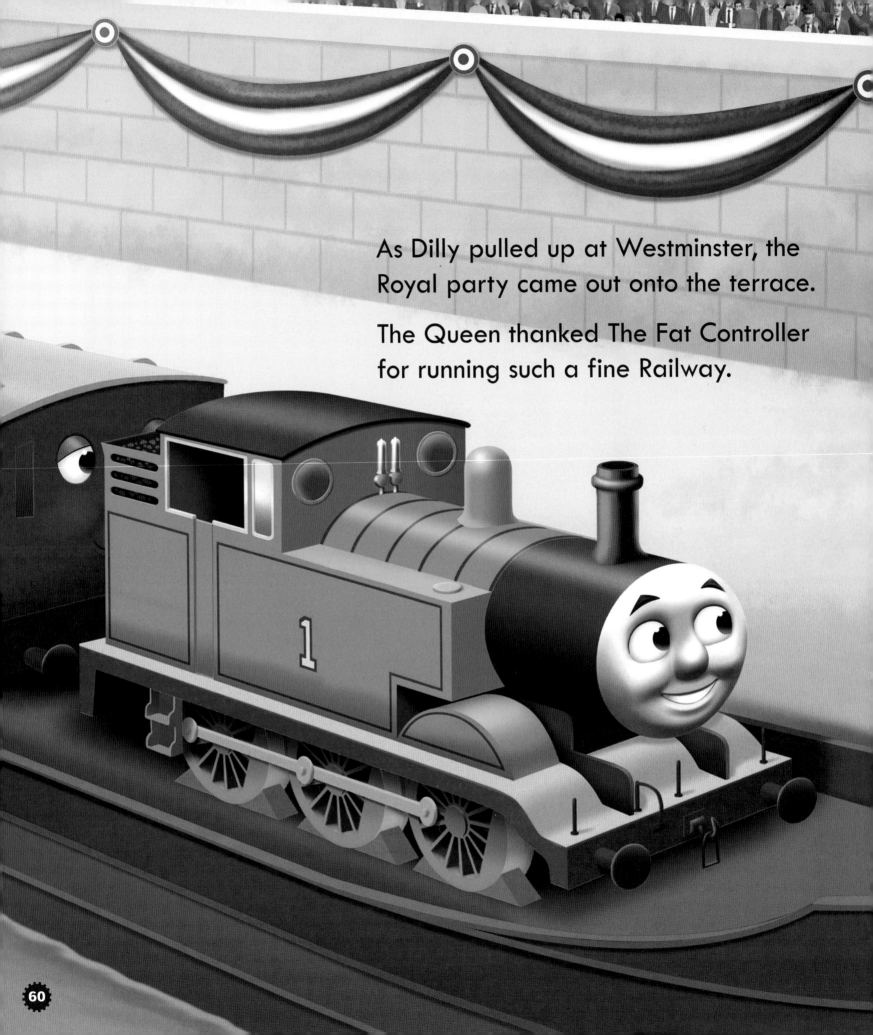

As Dilly pulled up at Westminster, the Royal party came out onto the terrace.

The Queen thanked The Fat Controller for running such a fine Railway.

"I couldn't do it without Thomas and my other Really Useful Engines," replied The Fat Controller.

Thomas beamed from buffer to buffer.

That evening, as Thomas, Annie and Dilly rested on the Thames, brilliant fireworks lit up the sky.

CRACKLE! WHOOOOOSHH! BOOM!

Thomas couldn't wait to tell his friends on Sodor about Big Ben, meeting the Queen and everything he'd seen in the biggest city in the land.

THREE CHEERS FOR
Thomas *the Tank Engine*

This is a story about Thomas the Tank Engine and the day when all his friends showed him what a very special engine he was...

One sunny day on the Island of Sodor, Thomas was running late.

"Go faster, go faster!" grumbled his coaches, Annie and Clarabel.

"I'm trying, I'm trying," puffed Thomas, but his wheels felt all wrong — they were stiff and sore.

69

The next day was no better.
Thomas was late to be coupled up to Annie and Clarabel...

late delivering
goods trucks...

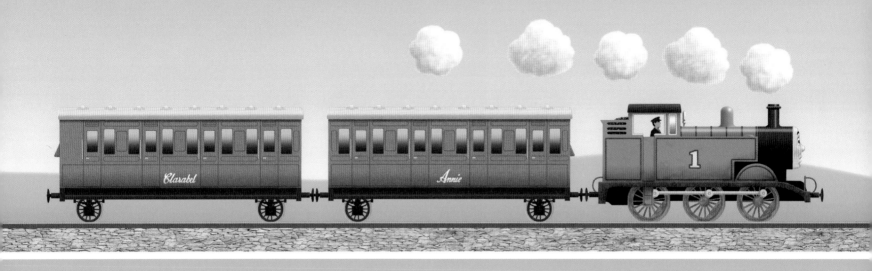

late shunting trucks...

...and late to the Washdown at the end of the day.

It was the same story all week.

Normally Thomas loved to race with his friend Bertie the Bus but on this day Thomas was too tired and his wheels were too sore to rush about.

"Not today, Bertie,"

said Thomas.

That night, Thomas puffed back to the Sheds, very slowly and very sadly.

Everyone was worried about Thomas. He was normally such a **cheerful little engine.** Nobody liked seeing him so sad.

"I remember when I had my **old, rusty pipes,**" said James. "I felt so slow and tired. I used to get out of breath, even on the shortest journey."

So the Engines decided to talk to The Fat Controller to see what could be done.

"Thomas' wheels are **rusty and worn**," The Fat Controller said. "We'll give him a **special day** with new paint, new wheels and a **surprise party** to celebrate!"

"With new wheels, Thomas might be *faster* than you, Bertie," teased Emily.

"Never!" tooted Bertie.

The next day The Fat Controller went to see Thomas.

"Today," he said, "you won't be pulling Annie and Clarabel. I'm sending you to the **Sodor Steamworks**."

"I understand," thought Thomas, sadly. "I'm not good enough to pull coaches. I'm not a Really Useful Engine."

And he **puffed** off to the Steamworks feeling very sorry for himself.

But at the Steamworks Thomas was given a smart **new coat of paint**...

...his dome was **polished**...

...his buffers were **buffed**...

...and he was given **brand new, shiny wheels!**

"Perhaps The Fat Controller thinks I can be a Useful Engine after all," said Thomas.

"I certainly do," laughed The Fat Controller, arriving to inspect the work. "You look ready for your party."

"My party, Sir?" exclaimed Thomas.

Thomas was about to puff off to
his party at Knapford Station when
Bertie pulled up next to him.

"Let's race to the party!"

Bertie said. "It's time to test out those special new wheels."

Bertie pulled away **more quickly** than Thomas and took the lead.

But Thomas' new wheels were turning *faster* and *faster* and *faster*.

He was catching up.

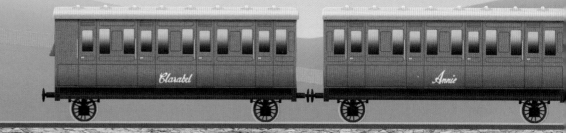

And when Bertie stopped to let some ducks cross the road, **Thomas overtook him!**

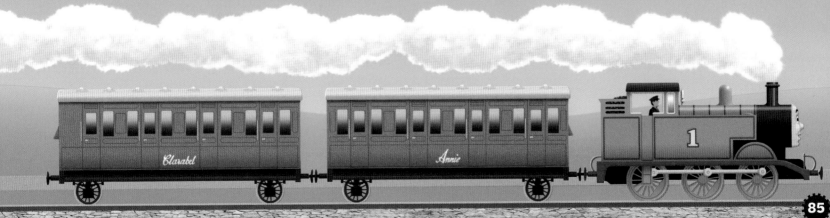

"Three cheers for Thomas!" said The Fat Controller, as they arrived first at the party.

"Hip hip hooray!
Hip hip hooray!
Hip hip hooray!"

"I just couldn't keep up with those new wheels," Bertie said as he pulled up.

It was a **wonderful party**! All Thomas' friends congratulated him on winning the race. Then they admired his new coat of paint and his shiny new wheels.

"Peep! Peep!"
Thomas tooted happily.

"I'm happy Thomas is back to his old self," said James to Bertie that night.

"Yes, it was fun racing him," smiled Bertie. "But next time he might not be so lucky!"

But Thomas didn't hear any of this, because he was already fast asleep.

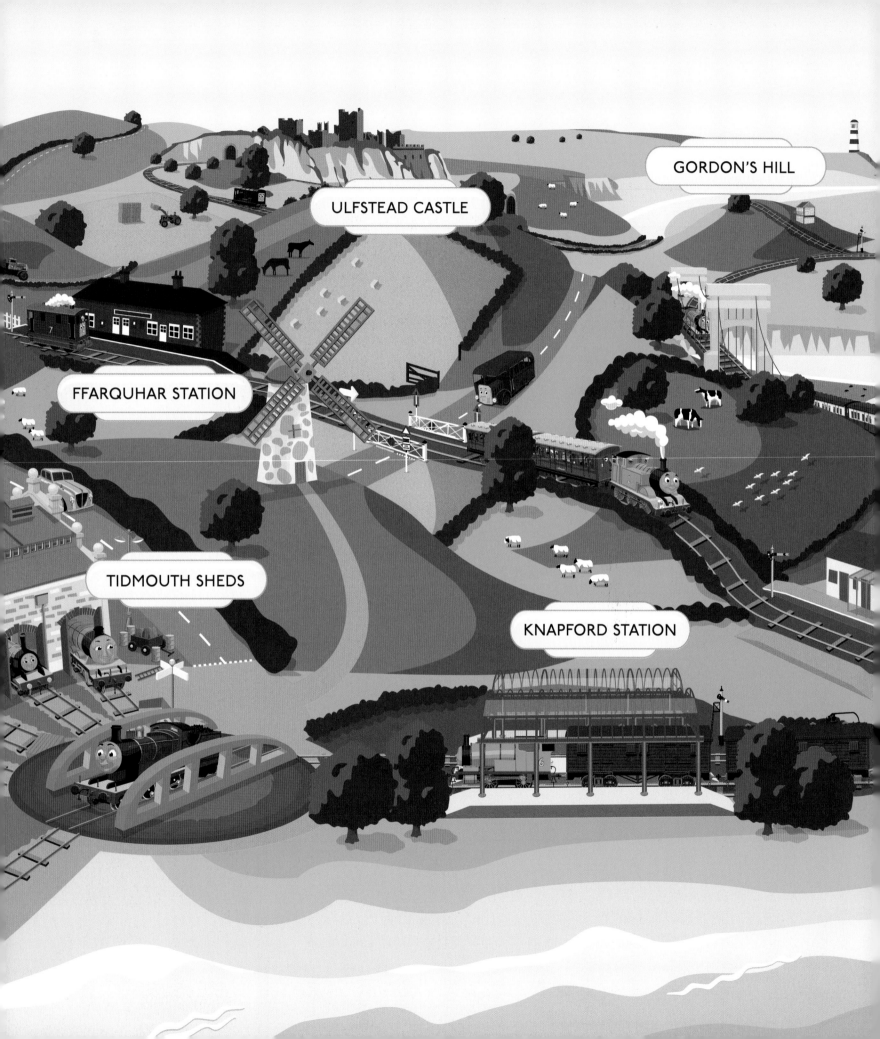

GORDON'S HILL

ULFSTEAD CASTLE

FFARQUHAR STATION

TIDMOUTH SHEDS

KNAPFORD STATION

BRENDAM DOCKS

CHINA CLAY PITS

DRYAW STATION

THE ISLAND OF SODOR

About the author

The Reverend W. Awdry was the creator of 26 little books about Thomas and his famous engine friends, the first being published in 1945. The stories came about when the Reverend's two-year-old son Christopher was ill in bed with the measles. Awdry invented stories to amuse him, which Christopher then asked to hear time and time again. And now for over 70 years, children all around the world have been asking to hear these stories about Thomas, Edward, Gordon, James and the many other Really Useful Engines.

The Reverend Awdry with some of his readers at a model railway exhibition.

The Three Railway Engines, first published in 1945.